FOUNTAIN OF YOUTH

R.V. PARK

R.J. BENETTI

Copyright © 2023 by R.J. Benetti

Edited by Nicole Walkow

All rights reserved.

No part of this book may be reproduced in any form or by any electronic or mechanical means, including information storage and retrieval systems, without written permission from the author, except for the use of brief quotations in a book review.

FOUNTAIN OF YOUTH R.V. PARK

The creature's heft denoted a time before man. The thing was a vestige, an anachronism, given new life. And it huffed. And it grunted. And it was... a brachiosaurus.

Its almond-shaped head jutted nearly parallel to the mountains in the distance.

Simply by walking, it stamped SUV-sized tattoos upon the dusty Wyoming landscape, then, it suddenly stopped, and it stared, keeping focused on a small dot traversing a winding road below.

The dot, if one were to zoom in, was a jostling bus filled to the brim with tourists, snapping photos, chitchatting excitedly, looking at their phones.

"Now look at that, folks!" said the scrawny tour guide, his voice bellowing through the bus's speakers.

He pointed to a pterosaur, spreading its wings to blot out the orange sun of a sapphire sky. It dipped its angular head down to direct its course through the air.

Zipping, soaring, it was the size of a private jet.

A little further off, the tour group could see a herd of triceratopses milling about and grazing on some dry brush.

"This is incredible! Absolutely, incredible!" a middle-aged, wiry haired woman named Deedee shouted.

Her husband, a bald, stout man with a thick mustache nodded agreeably beside her. His name was Norman, but his wife called him "Major." She instructed everyone else to do so as well—due to his years spent in the Army.

Major cleared his throat.

"Do they have any idea why the dinosaurs have settled in this specific area of Wyoming? I mean, why Hot Springs County? Why Thermopolis?"

The tour guide grinned, revealing his buckteeth.

"Great question, sir!"

"It's Major, not, sir!" sniped Deedee.

The tour guide winced, then glanced at his shoelaces. "Oh, right, Major! Sorry about that." He looked up again, regaining that steadfast showmanship that'd won him his job.

"Most of the world believes the dinosaurs came with the mineral water!" he continued. "That is, the mineral water had their paleo-DNA in it, or primordial fluid, like gigantizoid-reptile-jism, you know what I mean?"

Major scratched his forehead.

"You see, in 1918 a man by the name of C.F. Cross drilled into the ground in search of oil. Instead, as fate would have it, he struck a thermal hot spring! It'd been hibernating untouched ever since the Triassic or Jurassic period. And with a long yawn that was really a shriek it shot from the earth with such power it destroyed the drilling derrick."

"Fascinating," said Major, he looked to his wife, hoping to share the moment. Deedee gave him a dirty look.

"Yessir. Even burned some people's skin off since it comes out at 170 to 190 degrees Fahrenheit. People say that since the water is hundreds of millions of years old, it brought with it creatures that—"

BANG!

A sudden bump in the road cut off the guide's explanation.

Major crimped his brow, looking to his right. His two children, Davey and Samantha, were rubbing fingertips to the glass of their phones, scrolling through inane chats on obscure internet forums.

He nudged them with his wide knuckles and motioned outside to a pack of sprinting velociraptors. Samantha, the oldest, who was just beginning puberty, shrugged and creased her lips into a thin line.

While the youngest, Davey, didn't bother looking up. His shoulders danced with laughter at something someone said on a chat about his favorite video game, *Flamethrower's Gorilla Gauntlet 3*.

"Oh, wow! I feel like I'm tripping balls! Looks like the trees are even from way back then. Wild, man!"

The person speaking was tall and bearded. His beer-guzzler's paunch stretched the limits of his tie dye shirt; a shirt that had a heliotropic smiley face wearing an American flag bandana emblazoned in its middle.

Major stared at the man's tiny grey ponytail, the size of a pointer finger, swaying with the divots in the road. Like the creatures outside, this person was a vestige of a bygone era. The freewheeling, promiscuous, acid-dropping sixties.

"Check out the trees and bushes, man! They're all gnarly!" he blurted, glancing at a Korean couple sitting behind him to brandish his yellow teeth.

"Right you are!" said the tour guide. "What's your name, buddy? Have you been here before?"

"The name's Howard, but you all can call me Howie. And nope, never been!" Howard surveyed the bus.

He noticed a fine-looking middle-aged woman sitting near the back window; she saw him staring and mouthed the word *NO*. He narrowed his eyes on her for a moment and turned back to glance at everyone else.

They all promptly avoided eye contact.

So, Howard chose to focus his attention on the plants once more—their supersized fronds swaying with the arid breeze of the landscape. He couldn't help thinking that the plants looked like mutated marijuana. Howard smiled, pleased with his thought.

A few rows back from Howard, sat a wrinkled nonagenarian named Deloris. She was traveling to the R.V. Park with the hopes of a liquid panacea to cure her aches and pains.

It was she, and only she, who noticed something peculiar transpiring in the panorama—as if dinosaurs in the middle of Wyoming weren't odd enough—one of them, a lone stegosaurus, was stomping its feet in a spongy thermal puddle.

The dinosaur kept pointing its snout skyward, its toothy maw agape, roaring something to the clouds. The creature's look was unmistakable.

She'd seen it many times before, having outlasted two husbands and having reared four children... one of which she planned to see after the trip to the hot spring. Her favorite son, whose name was Daryll, sold cactuses in Las Vegas, Nevada.

The stegosaurus was clearly upset, vexed at something in its life as a thing of the *past* brought into the *present*. Deloris felt compassion for the spiked, 6,800-pound reptile.

She wished she could hug it. But then re-recognized its fury as it stamped the multicolored ground, warped by the hot mineral water. It felt good having distance between them.

"This is exciting, yah?" said someone, in a thick German accent.

Deloris turned toward the voice; it was coming from behind and over the aisle to the left. A brown-haired stranger smiled, his plump cheeks punctuating his friendliness. Deloris returned his congeniality with a smile of her own.

"I've been to hot springs all over de world," the German

said. "Good to loosen de body and release de pressure points in de fascia. Ja. Ja. This one at the R.V. Park supposed to be de best. Ja. I can't wait to play tennis again!"

"Tennis? I just want to be able to walk upright again without this darned thing." Deloris tapped the metal walker occupying the seat beside her. The stranger's lips abruptly curved downward, into a frown.

"But I do hear it's the best." Deloris smiled once more, attempting to steer the conversation to the Pollyannish cheeriness the German expected. "At least that's what it says in the ads."

"Ja. Ja. It says that. And if doesn't work, at least we were able to see some dinosaurs! Wunderbar!"

Deloris nodded, then pivoted to sneak another glance at the vista out of time. She searched for the stegosaurus, but he (or she) was gone.

As they sped toward Fountain of Youth R.V. Park, bouncing on asphalt cracked and rutted by the meandering of dinosaurs, each individual on the bus held their own separate vigil in the special place of their minds.

"We are almost there, folks! And if you'll look up and to your left, you'll see a little marker we've left for ourselves." The guide pointed to a tall grass-laden hill on which a series of dove-white stones was lined, spelling the following:

Welcome To Thermopolis
Home To Dinos & Hot Springs!
HOPE YOU ENJOY YOUR STAY!

Crunching forward, the bus neared a timeworn, little house inside the R.V. Park. A smoke-colored Pomeranian yipped as the wheels slowly stopped turning, pulverizing some final pebbles under their weight.

Outside of the bus, rows upon rows of green-grassed plots were arrayed with luxury Airstream campers parked in their driveways.

And outside of the fenced-in R.V. park, a 23-foot dilophosaurus extended its polka-dotted neck frill and hissed at a fumarole—a hole in the ground that emitted sulphureous steam that smelled like rotten eggs.

"We're here, folks! Welcome to the Fountain of Youth R.V. Park!" the tour guide announced, pulling a lever to open the bus's door.

Major assisted Deloris with her walker, while the German, Tobias, jostled to the front of the line, shoulder-bumping Howard as he did so.

"Whoa! Chill. What's the rush?" asked Howard.

But Tobias didn't answer.

The group exited, person by person by person, shuffling to the side of the bus where they could retrieve more luggage from the underfoot storage.

The outside air lingered both hot and dry, having that distinct, flatulent smell only dinosaurs and hot springs can create.

Davey and Samantha jumped down, alternating their attention from their phones to their bickering with one another. Deedee ambled close behind, exhibiting a plastered-on smile usually reserved for the most disturbing of mannequins.

They all grabbed their bags—Howard's being a rucksack made of moldering hemp.

From there, the group was lined up and ushered into the dilapidated "lobby" of the tiny house, whereupon they spotted a desk, behind which stood a wrinkled and swarthy Caucasian couple grinning from ear to ear.

They wore sweat-salted, bent-brimmed baseball caps and ratty yet comfortable attire. The man handed the tour guide a bottle of water and a few bills from his chiming register.

Nodding at his employer and the group he'd transported, the driver bid his nonverbal farewell with a slight clicking sound made from sucking the insides of his cheeks.

"Welcome, campers! My name is Jedidiah Beulah and I'm the owner of this here establishment! Along with my wife, Darleen, that is."

"Hiya, everyone! Ya'll are sure in for a treat!" said Darleen. "This is the best hot spring in all of Wyoming, and the only hot spring in the world to have real live dinosaurs in all their glory!"

"Yessir, that will be three-hundred dollars," whispered Jedediah to the German.

Tobias nodded, "ja, ja," and proffered his cash to the owner.

"Your camper will be right around the bend, third shiny, silvery thing to the left."

Jedidiah reached around an array of empty water bottles and pulled out a faded, retro-looking map from under his desk. It was manilla, with small areas of blue and red ink filling in some of the letters.

A tiny stick figure was doing a cannon ball from the R in R.V. Park. With permanent, black marker, Jedidiah made a large X on a cartoon plot of land.

"Remember the hot pools don't open until seven o'clock tonight. I expect you all to be there so we can show you the ropes!"

"Vunderful, ja!" Tobias held his map up in triumph. "I hope to be relax like a jelly!"

"Then jelly it is, I'll tell the springs to hold the peanut butter," Darleen interjected. "Enjoy your stay!"

Tobias walked off, mumbling, with confusion twisting his face.

Next, Major helped Deloris to the counter while his wife, Deedee, tried to corral the children since they were punching one another.

"There you go, ma'am," said Major, his mustache seesawing with every consonant.

"Thank you, you're a very kind young man," said Deloris, in her polite way... even though Major was easily in his middle to late fifties, with the appearance of a circus strongman.

Major nodded, his bald head shining from the overhead lights, and walked a few paces to join his family, including Deedee, who gave him another dirty look.

"That will be three hundred dollars, ma'am." Jedidiah held his hand out.

"Before I pay," intoned Deloris, clutching her purse with old fingers, "Can these waters really cure people's ailments?"

"Yes ma'am! These specific waters have miraculous life-giving properties. That's why they resurrected them dinosaurs out yonder... and I personally know, that they can reinvigorate your health and well-being too. You done came to the right place, and that's darn tootin!"

"But I have rheumatoid arthritis."

"We can treat it."

"And I'm a diabetic."

"Not no more, you ain't!"

"I also have stage three colon cancer."

"Consider it vanquished!"

Tears welled and rolled into the wrinkles beside Deloris' eyes. She slowly opened her purse. Jedidiah held out his hand.

"Three hundred, flat rate," he said.

She paid the man.

Next, Jedidiah collected the payment from Major, with the kids being given a special rate, which was really just a 20 dollar discount.

As Major was paying the fee, Samantha smacked the back of Davey's head, and Davey responded by chasing her out of the small house and into the R.V. Park.

Half-heartedly calling after them, Deedee grumbled then pursued her kids out the front door.

Howard, the hippie, laughed and made eyes at the woman he'd spotted in the bus. She shook her head, as if to say, *not in your wildest dreams.*

Nodding, Howard stepped to the front desk, dazed with a slight smirk.

"Bitchin place you got here, man!" he said. "I really dig it. It's got a cabin-y sort of feel but it's far out in some prehistoric thingmajig, or whatever you call it."

"Aw, thank you!" chirped Darleen.

"No problemo. You know I came to the Fountain of Youth R.V. Park as part of a vision quest?" he said.

"Is that right?" responded Jedidiah. "Well, we got the best visions. You ever see a Spinosaurus devour a sauropod from the comfort of an Olympic-sized hot tub?"

Howard smirked wide.

"Now you're talkin my kind of English! I also got this nagging back pain... I slipped off a slick stone hooking some buddies up with an inner tube. I run an inner tubing business on the river back home in the mountains of Idaho. So... you know I'm good for the green stuff."

"You're going to have to pay up front. And you're going to have to pay in cash, like it says in the advertisements, honey," said Darleen.

"Yep," added Jedediah.

"In my line of work, I don't just peddle any ol' inner tubes. My tubes are big ass tubes. They're the Cadillacs of inner tubes, or Rolls-Royces."

"We take cash here, not anecdotes." Jedidiah extended his hand.

"No cash, no once in a lifetime relaxation…" said Darleen.

Howard's face screwed up under his beard. He slid his hemp rucksack off his drooping shoulders, gently placing it on the floor. Doubling over with a grunt, Howard began rooting around in the bag until he erected his spine once more and stuck his long arms out.

Swaying in the clutches below each furry fist, were big Ziplock bags stuffed with change, pocket lint, a smattering of paperclips, bunched-up bills, a few tokens from arcades, Canadian, Mexican, and Uruguayan coins, and those novelty pennies that were flattened in random machines in random corners of the country.

"I told you I'm good for it," said Howard.

"Looks like you are…" responded Jedediah.

The Korean couple behind Howard started fidgeting—they tapped their feet on the worn carpet and the man anxiously fiddled with his sunglasses.

The woman Howard had continually made eyes at let out an exasperated sigh, rushing outside to smoke a Pall Mall.

We're almost at the finish line, Tina thought to herself, lighting up her slim.

Although the outside had been nice, the inside of the camper was untidy and unfurnished and gave one the sense that it'd never been dusted.

Deedee maneuvered her fingers through her brittle bleached hair and scratched at her scalp with her long, pink nails.

Her face was palsied with anger. They'd come to the Fountain of Youth R.V. Park to mend their marriage, and, once again, Major had messed it all up.

Major could sense her *SEETHING*. Remembering his Survival, Evasion, Resistance, and Escape military training, he tried his best to extinguish the powder keg that was his wife.

"Oh well… I guess you pay more for the thermal spring and the dinosaurs than the camper," he remarked.

Deedee snatched a paper plate off the floor of the R.V., exposing a previously hidden condom wrapper, with something akin to blood smeared upon it.

"Don't you look at me with your scared, little beady eyes right now, Major!"

"I—I—…"

Suddenly, Samantha slapped Davey across the mouth with a neck pillow, causing little flecks of spit to mist the peeling, wood-paneled microwave. Davey pounced, the two began grappling, each of them screaming obscenities and trying to pull each other's hair out from the root.

"It looked nicer in the pictures. Honestly, sweetie, it did…" Major's voice waned in the cacophony of fighting.

He hoped in a few hours the thermal spring would save this trip. Otherwise, the camel's back had finally snapped, and this *vacation* was the straw that did it.

Deloris sat at the foot of her bed in her camper, enjoying the tidiness of it all: the frilled-floral curtains, the spotless coffee maker, the fluffy towels with the dinosaur etchings. She smirked a wizened smirk.

Leaning forward, she continued to rub ointment on her calves and thighs as she mumble-prayed to herself, invoking the names of her dead husbands.

"Let this be the trick that does it, Handsome Henry.

"Let us heal these wounds like Jesus Christ healed those stricken with blindness, my sweet, sweet Malcolm.

"There's a lot of whites here, my dear, lovely Henry, hee-hee… some strange ones too.

"I met an odd German, like the ones you fought in the great war… hee-hee, I don't think you'd like him very much…

"Malcolm, do you get enough sleep up there? You always worked so hard… Oh boy, if you could see the creatures Malcolm, it's like nothing you would ever imagine…

"Yes, the kids are fine. I'm going to go see Daryll once I heal my cancer…

"Well, I love you both too," she said.

Howard sat in a lounge chair under his camper's canopy, enjoying a warm beer and gazing out and up at the twinkling stars emerging in the new night's sky. His mind was emptied of all worries, and for a brief moment, he felt truly sublime.

He dug in his pocket and pulled out half a joint, then grinned a deep yellow and snuck a glance over the small-pebbled road, noticing the lights on in Tina's camper.

In just one hour, they'd all take a dip in the miraculous

spring. Then, he'd offer Tina one of the two inner tubes he brought with him on this trip.

She'd laugh at his hilarious jokes—the ones where he compared the inner tubes to luxury automobiles—he'd offer her a joint, she'd say *of course baby*, then they'd go back to his place for a warm beer, then they'd move the party inside…

This is the life… Howard mused, leaning his chair back, hearing the faint cry of a tyrannosaurus rex in the mountains.

Tobias puttered to and fro in his pill-shaped aluminum alloy camper. Wearing only a speedo, the skimpiness of the article left the unflattering nature of his body fully exposed.

He was bizarrely shaped—with a rather large stomach, sagging breasts, thin arms and legs, and wide hips. Tobias applied a bronzer to the entirety of this strange frame and mustache wax to his overpowering eyebrows.

He glared at his reflection in the mirror, struck a few poses he'd seen in a Mr. Universe documentary, and said, "*Oh, Ja!*"

It was time to take a dip.

Tina placed the four-point seven-inch Berretta 950 under one of her impressive fake breasts. She studied her reflection, paying close attention to the lay of the red bikini on her skin.

The gun was fully hidden; fully concealed.

And, she assumed, most, including the creepy hippie, would only focus on her bustiness in the Baywatch-esque swimsuit. Her plan might work. They'd all be none the wiser that she'd come to the R.V. Park after her husband had vanished from it months before.

She'd even spoken to Jedediah and Darleen on the phone, and again, when they met in person in the quaint reception area, but they failed to recognize the distinct, tired lilt in her voice.

"We're so devasted by the event and sorry to tell you," Darleen had said. "Your husband was eaten by a flock of microraptors."

"*Micro...* what?"

"Microraptors," said Darleen. "Four-winged, two-foot raptors that fly around ravaging. Your hubby, being the paleontologist that he was, had ventured out yonder by his lonesome."

"What!? Why wasn't anyone there to protect him?"

"We would've if we'd been there, believe you me, we always advise against going out alone. Tour guide found his bones *and* his belongings picked clean. When he approached, the feathered freaks flew off in a terror. I'm so sorry to tell you about this... in this way..."

"We've never lost anyone before," added Jedediah, on the speakerphone. "It's a real loss for all of us."

After some one-sided sobbing, the owners of Fountain of Youth R.V. Park hung up the receiver on their end.

Tina was left with so many questions. Questions that she, herself, would have to answer.

Researching missing persons records, making innumerable phone calls to police, and family members of those who'd disappeared, as well as anyone else that could provide information, Tina found that her husband wasn't the only visitor to never return from the R.V. park.

In fact, there were *A LOT* of people that never came back.

Therefore, she'd come to the tourist destination to not only exact revenge, but to get some answers.

Suddenly, a voice, Jedediah's, could be heard through the Park's speaker system—rigged up atop all the wooden lampposts.

Tina snapped back to the present moment.

"Five minutes to seven, folks!" Jedediah said. "We're all ready for ya at the Fountain of Youth hot spring! If you'll put on your rubber duckies and head on down, we've got the soak of a lifetime waiting just for you!"

"Do we ever!" added Darleen.

Tina gently probed the gun hidden under her left boob. She braced herself, tried to erase the fury from her expression, and opened the camper's door. She smelt the night air, the sulphurous stink pumping from the thermal springs, and she smelt... the dinosaurs.

The visitors gathered at a chain link fence beside Jedediah and Darleen's unimpressive home-reception area.

Tobias was doing some calisthenics, side bends and squats, which made Deloris uncomfortable as she puttered forward with her titanium walker.

"Hi there," she said.

"Hallo! Ready to soak away your knots? Ja!" responded the German.

Deloris smiled and nodded, mumbling in the affirmative.

Nearby, Howard held large inner tubes with each of his arms, grinning a crooked grin and peering drunkenly through the swollen slits of his eyes.

He watched as Tina strutted up to the fence, avoiding his gaze, and everyone's gaze for that matter, focusing instead on the silhouette of the mountains surrounding them, and the cry of a stegosaurus, lamenting while wandering alone.

Deedee, Major's wife, was there too. Still fuming about the state of the camper, while the children, Davey and Samantha, played on their phones and compared the popularity of their social media posts.

Major, knowing his wife would take everything in a divorce, maintained his faux-chipper attitude.

He'd learned to be steadfast while traversing foreign battlegrounds, seeing friends blown to pieces by claymores or perforated by guerrilla bullets.

Keep calm, remember your training, and you might make it out of here alive, he'd always told himself, and did so again, on this night, solely out of habit.

Jedediah and Darleen moved as a nearly conjoined pair through their front door, conversing with one another as they strolled past the group. Howard couldn't help but think they looked more weather-beaten since the early afternoon, more worn by the elements and time.

Holding up his pointer finger, Jedediah slowly turned to face his customers.

"Hey, folks. There is only thing I would caution everyone on," he shouted. "There are three pools of varying temperatures. They are all fed by a spout that goes deep down into the earth and comes back out in the middle of that magical mineral formation yonder!"

Jedediah pointed through the gaps in the chain link fence, indicating a large cobalt, white, and yellow beehive-looking formation with water spurting from its top and running down its sides.

The water from the beehive coursed into a medium-sized pool, and the water from that pool drained into an even bigger pool, and the water from the even bigger pool drained into a pool roughly the size of the first.

"Don't go in the first one, or you'll get boiled like a Christmas lobster. And I'm talking boiled, and not *baked*, friend," Jedediah pointed at Howard, who didn't notice, since he was busy staring at Tina.

Stepping back, Tina tried to keep out of his line of sight.

"So, what you're saying is that the pools cool down, from one to the other?" asked Major.

"Exactly, you're a smart cookie!" Darleen responded.

Jedediah began unlocking the gate, turning the key in the keyhole, pushing it open.

"Enjoy your dip!" Darleen exclaimed.

Davey and Samantha sprinted through the gate, with everyone else following close behind. Davey toed the water, glancing around with a popeyed expression. "It's really hot!" he shouted, before his sister pushed him in.

Deedee was about to say something to get them to stop their roughhousing, but she buried her words within herself and decided to let it go. This would *all* be Major's problem soon, when she absconded for Tahiti, or Costa Rica, or anywhere, really, as long as it was far away from her family.

Tobias began wading into the coolest of the pools via a sloped access, an underwater ramp of sorts.

"Oh ja, so nice, ja, ja."

Howard dawdled a little behind and approached Tina. She looked everywhere, focusing one moment on Darleen and Jedediah Beulah circling the perimeter of the pools, and another on the supersized reptile cries in the distance.

"You look very nice tonight," said Howard.

Tina looked at him, her face a soft sheet of disgust.

"Can I interest you in one of these inner tubes? I can guarantee that they're the slickest in the country! It's like floating in a Ferrari!"

"Please, go away…" Tina said, rather curtly.

While Howard gawped at the side of her blonde-haired head, she studied the owners of the establishment. They were fiddling with the locks on the fence at the far end of the pool… behind the beehive mineral formation.

"What are they up to?" she whispered.

"Worried about the dinos?" asked Howard.

"I won't ask you again, leave me alone!" Her eyes relayed a finality Howard understood, a conclusiveness her words had failed to get across.

"Sorry, hope you find what it is you're looking for." Howard turned toward the pools, leaving her be.

Shrieking and giggling, Davey and Samantha splashed waves of thermal water into one another's squinting faces. Deloris moved away from them, keeping to the edges of the hot pool, letting the warmth comfort her old bones.

She stared up at the moon, hovering there, radiating the deepest, buttery hue.

It seemed so close she could almost taste it—the cornbread her sweet Malcolm used to make for her.

"I think I feel the cancer saying goodbye, Malcolm. I think it's had its fill and it's going…" she softly intoned.

Just then, Samantha jumped on her brother's head, submerging him in the liquid heat. Davey emerged, gasping.

Howard watched them, sniggering to himself, forgetting all about his rejection just moments before—the scene being so comical to his addled mind.

"Hey, do you kids want one of these inner tubes? This one here's like a Cadillac, it's just going to go to waste!"

The siblings side-eyed one another with a competitive flair and began freestyle stroking their way to the edge of the pool. When they arrived, Howard knelt down, his drinker's gut hanging over his faded neon swimsuit, his Hawaiian shirt unbuttoned, its loose flaps wafting the distinct scent of a burnt joint.

"Thanks!" Davey said, before snatching the inner tube. They paddled back out and continued wrestling like two eels in a hot tub.

With a sigh, Howard eased himself in, fully submerging himself beside Major, who was preoccupied in an odd conversation with Tobias.

"So, you're saying you've traveled the United States three times and you've never had a cheeseburger at the Roadkill Café off Route 60!?"

Tobias shook his head, indicating a *no*, and dunked himself, only to reemerge with a deviant's grin.

"I eat healthy, ja. I'm German but I don't even eat schnitzel! No meats!"

"Well, you've never had a T-Bone steak like the ones I cook!" said Major, thumbing his chest.

"Maan, I could go for a triple cheeseburger right about now!" said Howard, slapping his belly.

Major looked at him with revulsion. He was the sort of guy that spent his time suckling the U.S. government's teat dry of funds so he could go out bowling and hit doobies. He turned back to Tobias to continue the conversation, but the German was fully underwater, the only sign that he'd ever been there was a string of bubbles that popped on the water's surface.

Major glanced across the pool to Deedee, she was not only ignoring him, but everyone else. Deloris still seemed in the midst of her relaxed vigil, mouthing prayers to her deceased husbands, while Samantha and Davey partook in their brand of violent horseplay nearby.

Howard waded away from the retired soldier, his body jutting out from the middle of his donut-shaped inner tube.

Leaving Major all alone, with his thoughts.

Everyone swam in the hot pools now, engaged in their own separate activities, except for Tina, who, letting her rage boil over like the water spouting from the thermal formation, approached Jedediah and Darleen Beulah.

"Hi there, what can we do you for hun!?" chirped Darleen.

"My husband came this way a few months ago, we talked on the phone. This was the last place he was ever seen."

Jedediah shot his wife a quizzical glance.

"Don't reckon I know what it is you're talking about," he said.

"His name was—*is*—Northrop Tully. He's a paleontologist. You have to remember him!"

"Lots of people pass through these parts," said Darleen. "Could be, he just got a new lease on life, decided to desert you... after all, you seem to be getting up there in age."

Tina shook. It was all too much. These people were clearly lying to her. Glowering at the two of them, she went for her gun.

Just then, Davey started coughing. He held his hands to his throat, making gestures to show he was choking.

Major and his wife both panicked and started swimming to him.

Tina, meanwhile, leveled the weapon, but, being momentarily distracted, the husband-wife duo got the jump on her, shoving her into the hottest of the hot pools while she shrieked and fired a single shot toward the stars.

Howard would've defended her, if it weren't for his stomach. It was ballooning before his eyes, testing the limits of his inner tube. He tried to wriggle loose but the floatie continued to constrict as his stomach grew. A sharp, racking pain began to riddle his extremities. Howard was stuck, floundering.

At the same time, Deloris felt the cancer melt away, and

just as soon as she took her breath of relief, a new danger assailed her old body.

The names of her husbands and children fell from her lips.

She spasmed in the hot pool, coughing violently. Her posture corrected itself, then the vertebrae twisted into unnatural zigzags leaving her worse than before.

Seeing this, Tobias tried his best to swim to the access ramp, submerging and reemerging in pursuit of an exit.

As he swam, his arms began to tear from his torso—the tendons, ligaments, and muscles in his shoulders coming to resemble noodles in marinara.

With Davey still choking, Samantha screamed for her parents. Even though they were right in front of her… they seemed so very far away. Deedee trembled, narrowing her eyes on her husband. Major couldn't tell if she loved him. Never could. And it was even harder in that moment, with her face contorting.

"I righ here kids. I ri—gh, here, sweetie..." Major croaked, his voice slurring.

They all held one another as they morphed. Their bones popping, splintering, growing, reshaping, their human flesh bubbling and dropping off like wet bread from their awkward limbs.

Swatches of coarse green and black skin became visible through their torn flesh.

Howard couldn't speak, for he had no voice and the horns had already begun to split his skull asunder. He groaned, the jolts of hot-white pain hurt like nothing he'd ever experienced in his days as an inner tube salesman.

A studded frill of bone shot out from the crown of his head. Strings of blood and chips of bone misted the air.

An enormous appendage then punched its way through his tailbone, creating a large wave in the thermal pool.

Steam rose from the hot pools, and the humans mewled, their voices changing until they matched the timbre of that lone stegosaurus Deloris had seen from the bus's window.

A quartet of legs kicked from the inside out, through Tobias's guts, shredding his tanned-fattened stomach to fragmented flaps. His neck popped and grew, becoming the size of a large conifer.

Major huffed, spraying blood through a newly formed snout. His wife and kids did the same. They remained a unit. A familial pack of raptors, crowing and cocking their new heads.

Deloris, for her part, spread her wings, as the most magnificent purple pterosaur the owners had ever laid eyes on. Tina bubbled on the floor of her hot pool; her metamorphosis not yet evident to their waiting eyes.

With everyone's transformations almost being complete, Jedediah and Darleen unlocked the back gate and pushed it open.

"Let's git!" Darleen nudged her husband in the ribs.

"Hold on! I need ta see if the bitch still means us harm..."

Jedediah lowered himself, resting on his haunches at the lip of the hot pool. He unburdened a large, serrated bowie knife from his hip sheath, and he waited, as the waters roiled and churned.

"This is stupid..." said Darleen.

"Just wait, damnit!"

An eye surfaced from the boiling waters, tremendous in size and surrounded by a goop of leathery, crimson flesh. It was the eye of the predatorial giganotosaurus, larger and more deadly than any T-Rex. Its huge, forming teeth glimmered underwater, in the creature's monstrous jaw.

"Let's go," said Darleen.

But Jedediah didn't listen...

He just smiled and plunged his blade into the dinosaur's

pupil, sending a spurt of off-white goop in every direction from the perforation. The dinosaur, Tina, wailed for a brief moment with her new throat.

She sank like a cinderblock, to the pool's floor.

"It's too hot to make anything viable in there," said Darleen. "They done boil to death before they fully form..."

"Just hadta be sure," Jedediah responded.

The other sections of the pool swayed with heat devils and monstrous profiles, rising up from the primordial soup.

"Are you ready now?" asked Darleen.

Jedediah nodded.

They sprinted to their quaint home with grins twisting their leathery faces. Once there, they opened and shut the door behind them and rushed to their window, peering through the blinds with their smoke-colored Pomeranian.

They observed with greedy eyes, as a new group of tourist attractions writhed and wriggled to life.

"I think this was a good batch of dinos," said Jedediah.

"That it was," responded Darleen, keeping her attention focused on the scene outside.

Most of the creatures started to leave.

Howard the Triceratops trundled, confused.

Tobias the sauropod moved in small, sprinting starts.

The family of raptors clucked and nipped at one another.

Deloris, the Pteranodon, flapped her wings and shot off, still riddled with cancer.

AUTHOR'S NOTE

In the summer of 2020, I was still living right outside of D.C. With the coronavirus lockdowns, panic, and death, it was a congested, high-anxiety septic tank boiling over. Everyone was on edge.

And, since almost everything had gone remote, nothing was technically keeping me there.

So, my girlfriend and I, who lived in an even more populous area than I did, decided to go camping.

Across the country.

I jotted a few notes along the way, sponging up landmarks and sprawls of land I'd only previously seen in the movies. And, I especially made sure to remember any interesting individuals my girlfriend and I met along the way.

Many of the characters in this story are based on these interesting, very real people. I crossed paths with them during our *vacation*, which was life-changing, and seemed to be happening during the apocalypse.

Deloris, the old woman, ran an Air BnB outside of Chicago. She was an extremely nice, gentle widower, and she did have a son who sold cactuses in Las Vegas, Nevada.

AUTHOR'S NOTE

Howard, the middle-aged hippie, looked exactly as he was described in the story. He ran an inner tubing business in Lava Hot Springs, Idaho. And he did always talk about how his inner tubes were Cadillacs and Rolls Royces.

We met Major and his wife in a hot tub in Sedona, Arizona. She called him Major, due to his time spent in the military, and he really was a bald, stocky man with a large mustache. They didn't have any kids with them, however, and the wife, Deedee, was more of a cheerful wine guzzler than a spiteful spouse.

The other characters are just kind of a mishmash, especially the kids.

I saw these children everywhere, when the whole country was closed down, their parents tried to get them to stop arguing or to stop looking at their phones, to take a moment to absorb the splendor of America's state and national parks.

They never seemed to listen.

Oh well... back to the story.

You may be thinking, what happened to the Korean couple? They were in the bus, and they were in the reception area, being assigned a camper. Why weren't they in the transformative thermal hot springs in the end?

The answer is simple.

They took a nap, being exhausted and jet-lagged, and ended up oversleeping. Yep, that's my explanation! I totally didn't forget that they even existed.

Oh yeah, and Fountain of Youth R.V. Park is very real. A bit strange, and off the beaten path, it may or may not have had dinosaurs, but it was still one of the best places to have a soak!

Fountain of Youth
R.V. PARK

MasterCard
VISA
AAA

LARGE MINERAL POOL

IN THE ♥ OF big WYOMING

Printed in Dunstable, United Kingdom